CHLOE *by* DESIGN

*Un*RAVELING

BY MARGARET GUREVICH

ILLUSTRATIONS & PHOTOS BY BROOKE HAGEL

STONE ARCH BOOKS™
a capstone imprint   www.capstonepub.com

Chloe by Design is published by Stone Arch Books
A Capstone Imprint
1710 Roe Crest Drive
North Mankato, Minnesota 56003
www.capstonepub.com

Library of Congress Cataloging-in-Publication Data
Gurevich, Margaret, author.
Unraveling / by Margaret Gurevich ; illustrated by Brooke Hagel.
pages cm. -- (Chloe by design ; [3])

Summary: Having made it all the way through the Teen Design Diva
auditions, sixteen-year-old Chloe Montgomery and her long-time rival,
Nina, have arrived in New York where the rest of the competition will be
filmed — the contestants will face seven challenges, and the first takes
them to the Central Park Zoo.

ISBN 978-1-4342-9179-0 (hardcover) - ISBN 978-1-4965-0071-7 (eBook PDF)

1. Fashion design--Juvenile fiction. 2. Television game shows--Juvenile
fiction. 3. Friendship--Juvenile fiction. 4. Self-confidence--Juvenile fiction.
5. Central Park (New York, N.Y.)--Juvenile fiction. 6. New York (N.Y.)--
Juvenile fiction. [1. Fashion design--Fiction. 2. Reality television programs--
Fiction. 3. Competition (Psychology)--Fiction. 4. Friendship--Fiction. 5. New
York (N.Y.)--Fiction.] I. Hagel, Brooke, illustrator. II. Title.

PZ7.G98146Un 2014
813.6--dc23

2013048159

Designer: Alison Thiele
Editor: Alison Deering

Photo Credits: Brooke Hagel, 55

Artistic Elements: Shutterstock

Printed in Canada.
032014   008086FRF14

*Measure twice, cut once
or you won't make the cut.*

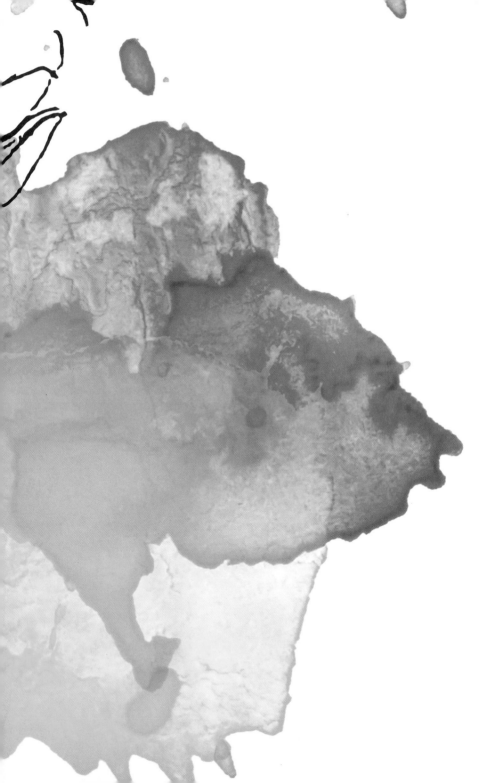

I'm finally here. New York City.

After I made it through the last round of *Teen Design Diva* auditions in California, everything was a whirlwind. I packed my bags, and my mom and I headed to New York City, where the rest of the competition will take place.

There's so much energy and craziness everywhere. The city is all taxis honking, people yelling, and lights flashing. It's different and scary, but thrilling too.

I look around our hotel lobby, the meeting place for the *Teen Design Diva* orientation. The letter delivered to my hotel room said all fifteen contestants should meet here. Everything looks so elegant — the marble floors, the plants hugging each corner of the room, and the soft, beige leather chairs. The other contestants are gathered nearby, and I recognize a few people from the earlier rounds of auditions, but the only person I really know is Nina LeFleur, a girl from back home. We're more rivals than friends, so I'm not exactly anxious to go talk to her. I wonder if everyone else is feeling just as nervous and excited as I am.

Just then, the elevator doors whoosh open, and the *Teen Design Diva* judges, Missy, Jasmine, and Hunter, walk into the lobby. They're followed by a camera crew. I've met them in person three times already, but my heart still starts to race at the sight of them.

Missy smiles warmly at all the contestants. "First of all, we'd like to welcome all of our talented designers to the Big Apple. Even if you're from New York City or have been here before, I guarantee this competition will be like no other experience you've ever had. When things get tough, remember to keep your eye on the prize — an internship with one of the city's top designers. It's an opportunity every designer dreams of, and it could be yours." With that, Missy waves Jasmine forward.

Jasmine's stilettos click on the floor, all business, as she steps to the front. "Let's get the important stuff out of the way. As I'm sure you know, you'll be in New York for one month. There will be a total of seven challenges, and two contestants will be eliminated after each challenge. The show will be taped, except for the final elimination, which will air live. All the challenges will be timed, and unless stated otherwise, you will be allowed to use only the materials we supply." Jasmine turns to Hunter. "Anything else you want to add?"

"Be creative," Hunter says, smiling at the group. "Use your strengths, but don't be afraid to try something new. Think outside the box."

At this last suggestion, I feel a poke in my back. I can't be sure, but it's probably Nina saying *I told you so*. That's exactly what she said the judges were looking for when she gave me that weird necklace before the final round of auditions in Salinas. Looks like she was just being nice after all.

"And remember," Missy adds, "have fun!"

"Your first challenge will be held tomorrow morning at nine o'clock in the Central Park Zoo," Jasmine tells us. "Your packets have maps as well as walking and subway directions. Don't be late."

* * *

The next morning, I'm up bright and early — partially because I couldn't sleep, but also because it was clear Jasmine wasn't kidding when she said not to be late. Seems like everyone else felt the same. All the other designers, along with their parents, gather outside the entrance to the Central Park Zoo at nine o'clock on the dot. The judges, producers, and camera crew are already there waiting for us.

"Fifteen for fifteen," says Jasmine, looking pleased. "We're off to a good start."

"For your first challenge, you'll have one hour to explore the zoo," Hunter says. "Decide what you'd like to see most. We'll meet back at the garden when you're done and explain more then. Choose wisely."

Everyone splits up to start exploring. My mom and I pass the zoo's Tropic Zone. Exotic rainforest birds chatter excitedly, and I make a mental note about the brightly colored feathers. As we move to the back of the zoo, monkeys screech at us from above as they swing from vine to vine.

I wonder how the zoo is supposed to play into our designs. Will we have to make clothes for animals? That would be a little out there, even for this show.

My mom and I come to a stop in front of the lion cage. Inside, the big cats are snoozing lazily. "They don't seem to be fully awake yet," Mom says.

I point to the description posted beside the cage. "It says they're mostly nocturnal. It must be too early for them too. Maybe we can come back."

We move on to the Polar Circle, and soon I'm watching polar bears, penguins, and other sea birds at play. The penguins waddle over to get a fish dangling from a zookeeper's hand, and the polar bears bat a huge ball around in the icy water. It's so easy to get lost in the animals' games. One polar bear does a loop around an ice tunnel and comes out the other end.

I notice some of the other designers gathering around and watching too. We all have notebooks and phones to jot down ideas, but none of us do. It's hard to know what to take notes on when we don't know what we'll be designing. From the corner of my eye, I see my mother glance at her watch and frown.

"How much time do I have left?" I ask.

"About fifteen minutes or so," she replies. "What do you want to do?"

"We should probably start walking back," I say. I'm a little nervous that I haven't seen enough yet, but I'm more nervous about being late.

My mom and I cut through the center of the zoo, past the sea-lion exhibit. Trees separate the area from the rest of the park. Small clusters of rose bushes bookend the trees — pink roses with yellow in the center, lavender ones with white accents, and red ones with white and yellow inside. In the center of the area is a large pool. Sea lions are sitting on the rocks around the water. Others are jumping into the pool.

"Sea lions are very social animals," a trainer is explaining to a group of contestants standing nearby. The sea lions bark and clap their flippers in agreement, and the trainer throws them a treat. Another sea lion does a flip in the air before diving back into the water.

A redheaded contestant claps his arms, sea-lion style, and the other designers and their chaperones laugh. "Where's my treat?" he calls. An identical redheaded boy standing beside him, obviously his twin, elbows him in his ribs.

As I watch, the sea lions race around the pool. Their sleek, dark bodies look elegant as they glide through the water like underwater ballerinas. A moment later I glance up and see the judges have gathered beside the rose bushes. Time's up. I can only hope what I saw brings me the inspiration I need.

I head over to where the judges are waiting, and the rest of the contestants follow suit. While we were exploring, the producers assembled several racks of clothing and a table covered with a sheet.

"Ladies and gentlemen," Hunter says, "you had some time to explore, and we hope you were paying attention. Because your first challenge will require you to use the animal exhibits as inspiration."

Oh, man, I think. *Maybe I wasn't that far off. Maybe they're going to make us design clothes for the animals after all.*

"Your challenge is to think about your favorite exhibit and create an outfit that reflects that," Jasmine says. "But there's a twist. Because there are no electrical outlets available to us here at the zoo, that means no sewing machines. This first task will simply be hand sewn."

I try not to groan. Of course there's a twist. It wouldn't be *Design Diva* without one. I should've known they wouldn't go easy on us just because it's the first challenge. Hand sewing will make things that much harder.

"You will be given three hours to complete your design," Hunter continues. He points to the rack, and I notice basic shirts, skirts, pants, and shorts — stuff I'd lounge around the house in. "As you can see, there's nothing glamorous about these pieces. But there could be. Your task is to change them from drab to fab. Add a fancy hem. Dress something up with ruffles. The sky is the limit as long as you make it work."

I try to take a deep breath and think clearly. Back when I first started sewing, I used to do this kind of thing all the time. Transform my clearance skirt with a cool embellishment or a funky hem. I should be able to come up with something in three hours, right?

"And last but not least," says Missy, "you'll be able to use all this!" She pulls the cover off the table to reveal dozens of fabrics and embellishments.

Around me, I hear the rest of the designers gasp. Whatever apprehension we have about this task is momentarily replaced with awe at the assortment of materials.

"Impressive, right?" Missy says. "Take it all in, but watch the time."

I ready myself, one leg in front of the other, as if I'm about to start a race. Jasmine raises her hand and looks at her watch. "Your time. Starts. Now!"

A handful of contestants run to the shelves, but I hesitate. How can I get started when I don't know which exhibit I want to focus on? The monkeys were kind of interesting. Not sure what I can do with them, though. The lions were promising, especially with their stunning fur, but all they did was sleep. Penguins? Polar bears? The sea lions?

I look around, trying to come up with an idea. I don't want to do anything too crazy since we have limited time and no sewing machines. Those constraints make things pretty difficult. Suddenly it hits me. The garden! I can make something inspired by the nearby flowers. It might not be animal-centric, but it *is* a zoo exhibit.

My idea starts to take shape as I browse the shelves and racks. A white T-shirt catches my eye. It's plain right now but perfect for this challenge. I grab it off the rack and start sketching. While I think of how to dress it up, a breeze picks up and the smell of roses hits my nose. I use colored pencils to add a ruffled collar — that will make the shirt stand out. I hold the paper in front of me. It definitely looks unique. In fact, it would be perfect — if I was designing for a clown. I bite my lip and check the clock. I have still have more than two hours left, but I want to make sure I leave myself plenty of sewing time.

Just then, a cameraman moves closer to me and zooms in to take a close-up of my disastrous drawing. I was so focused I'd almost forgotten about the cameras. I try to shield my paper a bit. That quick sketch is *not* how I want to introduce myself to viewers.

I stare at the plain white T-shirt in front of me. I definitely want to use ruffles to simulate the delicate petals of the flowers in the garden, but how to incorporate them? I don't want to do anything too cheesy or amateur. What if I ditched the sleeves? A halter top would look a bit more refined. And keeping it all one color would help.

I quickly eliminate the sleeves from my sketch and tweak the neckline. Then I add soft, white ruffles along the neckline in a bib design. They'll mimic the flower petals from the garden and also frame the face of whomever is wearing it.

I take a moment to study my sketch so far. Success! Now all I have to do is execute my design. With no time to waste,

I attack the shelves for supplies: needles, scissors, thread, and some white chiffon for the ruffles.

I pick a spot beside a tree and lay out all my materials. Cutting off the sleeves is the first step so that the creation doesn't look like some weird T-shirt hybrid. Then I can use the chiffon for the flower petals. I quickly create the new silhouette, then get to work hemming the frayed edges.

When I've finished that task, it's time to add the ruffles. They're what will really tie the shirt into the zoo's garden. I try not to think about my sewing machine back home. Things would be so much easier if I could use the ruffler foot on my machine. The special attachment creates ruffles in seconds and is one of my favorite machine-sewing tricks.

"One hour left," Hunter announces to the group.

Only an hour left! Where did the time go? I think frantically.

I quickly trace the shape I'll be cutting out onto the chiffon. The lightweight material is perfect — the movement of the material mimics the flower petals perfectly. I hold the chiffon up against the front of the T-shirt and think through my plan of attack. The ruffles need to have some volume, otherwise they'll just flop around. I start pinning the fabric in place, bunching the ruffles up so they don't lie flat, and start sewing. There's no time for fancy stitching. I just have to make things stay put. I attach them along the neckline and down the front. The rough edges of the chiffon give the shirt a cool, modern look. My fingers work quickly, and my wrist gets tired. I use a running stitch to make fixing mistakes easier, and it's enough to hold the ruffled petals in place. If I had more time, I would have used something sturdier, like a cross-stitch, but then I'd be stuck if I messed up.

"Thirty minutes!" Hunter says from behind me. I jump a little. *How long has he been standing there?* I wonder.

Hunter moves on, but now I'm feeling a little frazzled. The thread rips in my fingers, and I try not to panic. I can do this. I thread the needle again and try to concentrate, blocking out everyone around me and focusing on the thread and ruffle. In and out, in and out — ouch! Stupid needle.

A cameraman moves closer to capture what I'm working on. I try to stay focused, but it's almost impossible to ignore him. My needle moves quickly as I attach the rest of the petals. When I'm done I hold up the T-shirt and want to cry.

The ruffles look like they've been attached to the shirt haphazardly. The finished product barely resembles my original sketch. The petals are limp, and anyone with decent eyesight will be able to see the crooked stitching. The threading is straight in some spots and jagged in others.

"And time!" Jasmine calls.

I sigh. There's nothing I can do now except hope for the best. But I'm getting a little worried that my best might not be good enough.

FINAL
ZOO
Design

HALTER
TOP

RUFFLED
"BIB" MADE
OF CHIFFON
PETALS

WHITE T-SHIRT
REDESIGN

ELASTIC
GATHERED
HEM

Rose Garden Inspired!!

ANIMAL-INSPIRED
DESIGNS

HORIZONTAL
G RUFFLE T

BOW
RUFFLE
HALTER

LOOSE
PETAL

Keyhole

RUFFLE
HALTER

FABRIC
FLOWER
+LEAF
with stem
stitching

RUFFLE
"BIB"

Judgment time. I grab my lackluster top and join the rest of the contestants in a line in front of the judges. I have a feeling this is going to be painful.

Jasmine, Missy, and Hunter start at one end of the line. I peek around to see who will be first. It's a girl with dark hair and shockingly pink bangs. I think she was the one who used studs and jewels to liven up the rodeo uniforms in the last round of auditions.

"Daphne, tell us what you chose to make," Jasmine says.

"Um, I was inspired by the tropical rainforest," Daphne says, sounding a bit uncertain. She holds up a rainbow-colored pencil skirt that has feathers dangling from the hem. "Specifically all the tropical birds. I chose to liven up what was a plain Lycra skirt with bands of color and feathers."

"I appreciate your bold use of color, Daphne," Hunter says, "but I'm not sure the feathers are working for me. They're a bit much. I think this is a case of less being more."

The judges move down the line asking the same questions: *What inspired you? Why did you choose these colors?*

When they get to Derek, it's obvious he's blown them away with his creation — just like he did back in the final challenge in Salinas. His drab clothing of choice is an oversize purple V-neck shirt. He's managed to turn it into a chic dress with a loose, flowing purple top and a leather skirt on the bottom.

"It's inspired by two different areas," Derek says. "The children's zoo area and the sea lions. The different textures represent all the hands-on things in the children's zoo, and the faux leather fabric I choose for the bottom half of my dress reminds me of the sea lions."

When I crane my neck to study Derek's design, I see how seamlessly the skirt is attached to the shirt. It's a chic, color-blocked masterpiece.

"Very creative, Derek. Thank you," says Hunter, running his fingers along the stitches before moving on.

The judges are getting closer. They've made their way over to a girl standing a few feet away from me. I have a good view of her design, and it looks like it might be a kilt. Was it supposed to be a kilt? It's hard to tell because there is no obvious stitching on the plaid fabric she chose.

"Stefanie," says Missy, "tell us about your design."

Stefanie sniffles. "I had to unravel the whole thing," she says, looking at the ground.

Jasmine frowns. "So you just have the fabric?" she says.

"Yes," says Stefanie, "but I can tell you what it was supposed to be."

"That won't be necessary." Jasmine sidesteps Stefanie and moves on. "Luke," she says as she presses on her eyelids with her fingertips, "please tell me you were able to do something."

"I did something," Luke whispers, his shaggy hair falling into his eyes. "This was going to be a dress." He holds up a gray linen cloak with cross-stitching in the center, and I try to imagine the dress that could have been.

Jasmine takes another deep breath. It must be killing her not to lash out at Luke, but it's only day one. "But it chose to become a cloak instead?" she asks tightly.

"Yep," says Luke.

"Well," says Missy, "at least you have something that can be used, right?" She pokes Jasmine in the ribs, but Jasmine shakes her head and walks over to me, totally tuning out Luke's explanation about which exhibit he was inspired by.

As Jasmine comes to a stop in front of me, my heart starts pounding. The cameras focus on me, and I try not to look as panicked as I feel. At least I have something, right?

"What do you have, Chloe?" Jasmine asks. Her voice is desperate, like she's begging me not to disappoint her.

"I was thinking about the gardens all around us when I made this ruffled shirt," I say. "The chiffon ruffles I added to the neckline were inspired by the flower petals, and I opted to stick with white fabric to keep things clean and monochromatic."

Hunter nods. "I like that you reimagined the silhouette; you're one of the few designers to do so. I also appreciate that you've stuck with your style aesthetic in terms of the neutral color. And the stitching is very precise here."

I smile and nod as he, Jasmine, and Missy huddle together to inspect the shirt. *Don't panic*, I think. *Maybe they won't notice where you messed up.*

"But not so precise here," Jasmine says, pointing at the wild sewing.

Busted. I open my mouth to explain, but what can I say? I ran out of time? I messed up? I'm sure they can figure that out themselves.

The judges continue their critiques, and soon there are only five designers left — Nina and the two sets of twins in the competition.

Next to me, Luke scowls. "I thought we each had to make our own designs," he says.

What is he talking about? I wonder. *The twins didn't work together, did they? Wouldn't that be against the rules?*

Jasmine sends a stern look in Luke's direction. "Of course everyone is responsible for his or her own designs," she says. She turns back to the twin brothers. "Sam and Shane are aware of that, right?"

They nod, and Jasmine turns to the twin sisters beside them. "Jillian, Rachel? Separate designs each task." The girls nod too. "Splendid," Jasmine says. "Then let's keep going."

Sam explains that the polar bears' arctic exhibit inspired him to stitch embroidery on a simple white shirt. I leave my mannequin to check out his stitching. There is not even a smidge of faulty sewing. Each pattern is carefully crafted, and it's hard not to be jealous. It's simple but immaculate.

Not to be outdone, Shane took a pair of boring khaki pants and changed them into business shorts. "I was inspired by the trainers' outfits," he explains. He expertly stitched the hems to prevent fraying and added intricate embroidery to the belt area. If I didn't know better, I'd say the twins had a sewing machine stashed nearby.

"Fabulous," says Missy, unable to contain her excitement. "I love the idea of dress shorts. It's very European."

Sam and Shane fist bump and grin at each other. Next to them, Rachel and Jillian giggle nervously as the judges move over to inspect their pieces.

"I was inspired by the Arctic Circle as well," says Jillian, pointing to the bright blue, high-waisted skirt she created. "This originally had buttons and a zipper, which I removed to make it more elegant. I also added fabric to create a wrap belt and embellished it with crystal studs, which remind me of snow."

Before the judges can finish admiring Jillian's skirt, Rachel launches into her explanation. Jillian narrows her eyes at her sister, annoyed that she's stealing her spotlight. "My design," Rachel says, "was inspired by the lions." She added brown leather panels to a denim dress, giving it a jungle feel.

That's thinking out of the box, I realize. She didn't let the fact that the lions were sleeping stop her. She thought beyond that. Why didn't I?

"Very creative work, ladies," says Hunter. "And last, but certainly not least, Nina."

Nina looks confident, but I'm not sure if it's real or an act. "As you can see," she says, "I sewed a white shirt to a high-waisted black skirt to create a two-toned dress. It's an homage to the penguins."

Homage? I think, stifling a giggle. Definitely an act. Who talks like that? Just then I notice a camera focused on me. Oops. I hope they didn't catch me laughing at Nina.

Nina explains that she changed the crewneck collar of her shirt into a v-neck to help elongate the garment. The idea is similar to Derek's, but the designs are leagues apart. Where Derek's stitching flowed seamlessly, Nina's is visible and jagged.

The judges run their hands across the fabric, studying it quietly. Finally, Hunter says, "I can see where you were

JILLIAN'S SKIRT
WITH BOW

DAPHNE'S SKIRT
WITH FEATHERS

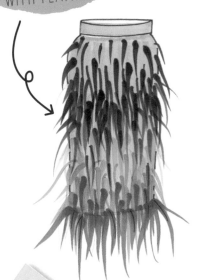

DEREK'S DRESS
WITH LEATHER SKIRT

going with this, Nina, but the execution could use some work. Your stitching is very uneven in a lot of places."

Nina nods, no longer smiling. I know how she feels, but I think we'll be safe for this round. The fact that our designs were finished should keep us safe from elimination.

"Thank you, everyone," says Missy. "The judges need to deliberate for a bit. When we come back, we'll let you know who's safe and which two designers will be sent home."

With that, Hunter, Jasmine, and Missy disappear into a nearby building. The rest of us look at each other, but no one says anything. I glance down at my design again. I really need to budget my time better for the next challenge. If watching *Design Diva* has taught me anything, it's that there are going to be lots of insane challenges. I'll have to learn to do what Rachel did and see beyond what's there.

Just then, the judges emerge from the nearby building. All the contestants look eager and nervous. Missy seems a bit dejected as she takes her place in front of us. "We understand this was the first challenge, and we wish we could have given you more time to get used to the process," she says, "but rules are rules."

Hunter nods. "We also know that what we see now will improve dramatically by the end of the competition," he says.

"However," Jasmine adds, "we have to work with what we have." She turns a page in her notepad. "In the top five, we chose designs that truly impressed us. Designs that didn't make us think, 'this could have been truly great with more time.'"

I swallow. My design is definitely not in this category.

"If I call your name, please step forward," Jasmine says. "Derek, Sam, Shane, Rachel, and Jillian — congratulations! You're in the top five. That means that in the next challenge, you'll have first choice of materials. You'll also be given extra planning and sewing time."

Sam and Shane fist bump, the girls hug, and Derek gives his dad a thumbs-up. I try not to groan. All five of them made amazing designs this round, and time wasn't an issue. I can't imagine what they'll create with extra sewing and planning time.

"Unfortunately, we also have a bottom five," Jasmine says.

I remind myself to breathe as she starts listing off names. In the bottom five are Stefanie and Julia, neither of whom finished their designs; Luke; and two guys named Tom and Curt. Thankfully, I'm safe.

"Again, we know the time constraints were hard," Missy says. "But we still have to let two of you go. Stefanie, Julia, because you weren't able to make any sort of design, you'll be leaving us today. I'm sorry."

As the eliminated designers step forward, I catch Nina's eye. She shrugs and makes a disappointed face. Stuck in the middle of the pack was not how either of us wanted to start off the competition. But right now, survival is what matters most.

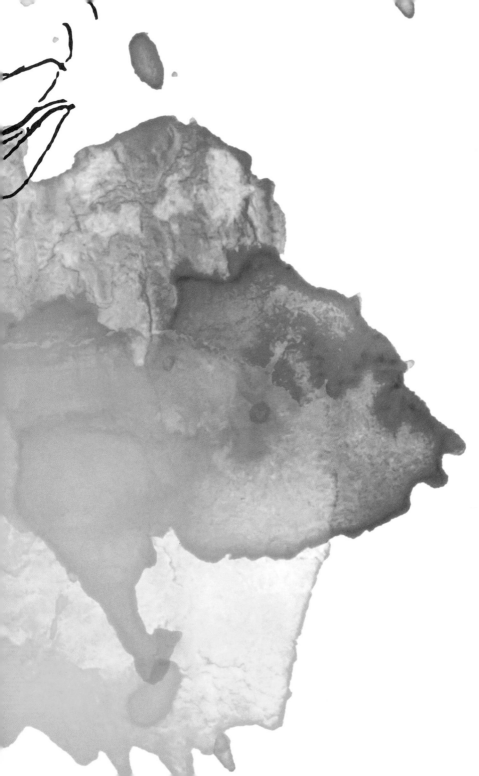

Two days after the zoo challenge, I sit in the hotel room, staring at the note that was slipped under our door early that morning. I read it for about the hundredth time.

"This can't just be a treat," I say. "It has to be the next challenge."

My mom sighs. "I know, Chloe, you've been saying that all morning. Why don't you go check it out already?"

I throw down the note and head downstairs. There are no judges to be seen, just hungry contestants and a towering display of mini cupcakes. They're all beautifully decorated in pastel frosting with gold and silver flecks along the edges. Edible pearls adorn each swirl.

I choose a dainty pink one. It takes two bites to finish. Next, I pick a green one with silver flecks. The taste is a surprise: key lime with custard in the middle. Yum! After two days of worrying about how I can get into the top five, this is a welcome break.

Speaking of the top five, I realize that Derek and the two sets of twins are nowhere in sight. Are they off strategizing somewhere? I wonder. I see Luke and the two other boys from the bottom five sitting together too. The reality shows I watch are all about forming alliances. Is that what both groups are doing? Should I be joining up with someone too?

Before I have time to worry about it, the judges arrive.

"Ladies and gentlemen," Hunter says, "I'm glad to see you're enjoying your treats, but on this show, things aren't always what they seem. And today, a cupcake is not just a cupcake — it's also your inspiration. For the next challenge, you will have to create cupcake-inspired headpieces."

"Headpieces?" Luke calls out. "I thought this was a clothing design competition."

"The best designers have range," Jasmine says. "We want to see yours. So if it can go on your head, it meets the requirements."

"Be creative," Hunter continues. "You have three hours to complete this task."

I still don't see the twins or Derek. Even if they are currently my biggest competition, it doesn't seem fair to have them miss this task.

Jasmine seems to read my mind. "Some of you may have noticed that the top five designers from the last challenge are missing. That's because as part of their prize, they got a head start. They're already at work behind these double doors."

I'd totally forgotten about that. Hopefully, there's still some good fabric left. My goal is to budget some planning time, then sew, sew, sew. But first, I need a design. What's cute and feminine like a cupcake? A bow! I can make a cool hat with a killer bow. In green. Like key lime pie.

Wait, is that too easy? I wonder. *No, don't overthink it.* I've seen plenty of *Design Diva* competitions where the contestants were so busy second-guessing themselves that they ended up with disastrous designs. Or worse — nothing at all.

Jasmine and Hunter walk over and open the double doors. The top five designers are already hard at work inside and don't even raise their heads when we walk in. They are too busy stitching — by hand. *No sewing machines again?* I think. This task keeps getting better and better.

In front of us, I see shelves covered with bolts of fabric. There are also sewing supplies arranged in baskets beside the shelves. It looks like there's one basket for each designer, so that will make the organization easier. At least I won't have to waste time racing around for supplies.

"I hope those cupcakes gave you some ideas," Hunter says. "Because time starts now."

I find a spot in the corner and whip out my sketchpad. I do a quick sketch, then run for the shelves. I'm almost there when someone elbows me hard in the ribs. I double over and try to catch my breath. When I look up, a camera is zoomed in on me. "I'm fine," I say to the camera, getting back up.

"Accident! Sorry!" Nina calls as she rushes back to her station with her supplies in hand. There's no time to wonder if she's telling the truth. I race to the shelves, and my eyes zero in on the shimmery green satin. I grab that, along with some lighter-colored scraps, a hat form, a needle and thread.

Since I know what my fabric looks like now, I add details to my sketch. I sit with the materials, trying to get a feel for the fabrics. My machine would have let me complete this task quicker, but this design is doable.

I grab a glue gun and carefully add glue dots to the satin before firmly pressing the lighter material to it. Then it's time to scrunch and sew. I squeeze the center of the fabric into an exaggerated bow shape and stitch the middle together so it will stay in place until I make a loop. I pull the thread tight with each stitch so the middle is sewed firmly.

"Ninety minutes!" Hunter calls out.

I can't believe half the time is already gone. The bulk of my headpiece is done, but I have to attach it to the hat form. While the glue gun is reheating, I sneak a look at what everyone else is making. Last week's top five designers are huddled in one area, sewing like crazy. Even with extra time, they don't seem close to finishing.

In another area, Nina looks like she's making some kind of clip, but when she sees me looking, she covers her design. Like I would copy her. The judges made it clear that identical designs would result in elimination. Then there's Luke, who looks like he's doing more eating than designing. There's a suspicious smear of frosting on his lip. Maybe he's just a fast worker and has extra time to eat.

Getting back to work, I measure the width of the hat form I chose and pick a piece of green fabric to cover it, making sure it's large enough to fully cover it. Then I wrap it around the form, attaching it to the underside with glue. Holding the ends firmly in place, I count to thirty in my head and then release my fingers. Once the fabric feels dry, I carefully attach the bow I created.

I glance up at the clock. Done, with five minutes to spare.

CUPCAKE
DEVELOPMENT
Sketches

FROSTING SWIRL
ELEMENT

INSPIRATION:
KEY LIME CUPCAKE

CUPCAKE
SHAPE

RIBBON ACCENT

FLOWER
FASCINATOR

"Nice bow," says Nina as we walk to the center of the room to display our designs.

I can't tell if she's being serious or sarcastic. "Thanks," I say, giving her the benefit of the doubt. I look at her design, a pink barrette decorated with small, red stones. "You too."

Nina doesn't say anything. Maybe she's too preoccupied with the judges, who are already fawning over Derek's hat, which is an elegant replica of a cupcake.

"Derek," Missy says, "I don't know how you put this together in such a small time frame, but I am impressed. There's minimal stitching. The rest is fabric spray? Glue gun?"

"Both," says Derek.

"Can't tell," says Hunter. "Good job."

It is an impressive hat. Now I'm really envious of the extra time the top five had. It clearly paid off. Luke is up next, and the contrast between the two designs is glaringly obvious.

"What," begins Jasmine, "is this?"

"A headband," says Luke. "It combines three different fabrics, which represent the different colored cupcakes, and can be worn inside out too."

Luke's idea is definitely simple. What he created probably took an hour max. Which would explain how he had time for his cupcake feast.

Jasmine holds up the headband and examines it. She flicks something off the material and makes a face. He even got frosting on the fabric.

The judges walk to the next competitors, and I look at Luke. He's smiling. I guess he figures as long as he's not eliminated, it's all good. I think of my dad's favorite expression: you can't have your cake and eat it too. Luke sure proved him wrong.

"Come on!" Jasmine is yelling. "That's just not acceptable!"

I crane my neck to see what she's so mad about. My mouth drops open when I see Beth's and Zoe's "designs." Both haphazardly sewed a few pieces of fabric together and then smeared cupcakes all over it.

"Explain," Jasmine sputters. "Now."

Beth grins. "It's an edible veil. It's called avant-garde."

Jasmine stares her down, but Beth doesn't blink. "And what's your story, Zoe?" Jasmine demands.

Zoe giggles. "Edible hat."

"It's like you two tried to outdo each other for worst creation," Jasmine says through clenched teeth.

When the girls say nothing, Jasmine looks like she's ready to storm out. Instead, she stalks over to Sam and Shane, the twin brothers who were in the top five in the last task.

"Can you tell us about your design?" Jasmine asks Sam.

"I call it the anti-cupcake fascinator," Sam says. "I focused on using shades of orange and black to add mystery. Then I attached fabric to the back to create a retro tie-back visor."

The way he combined his colors still makes me think of cupcakes, like side-by-side Halloween ones. Yet, he took the design to another level. He didn't see the pastel colors and think they were his limit. Maybe that's what will set his design apart.

"I really like that you didn't just take the task at face value," says Hunter.

Turns out Shane, Rachel, and Jillian didn't either. They did have more time than the rest of us, but thinking beyond the task is what sets their designs apart. Shane created a reversible knit hat and shaped the fabric to resemble a cupcake. Jillian constructed a headscarf with a 3-D cupcake design. It's not something I would ever wear. Not something *anyone* should wear. Ever. But I can't deny the high level of difficulty.

"My headpiece was inspired by the yellow-and-white cupcake," Rachel says. "The colors reminded me of a daisy so I created appliquéd daisies with pearl centers."

Missy inspects the small, hand-sewn flowers Rachel made and is clearly impressed. They're so precise, I have no idea how she completed them in the time limit. I am *not* looking forward to being judged after her. My hat and bow would have looked more impressive after Beth and Zoe's edible art.

"Hi, Chloe," says Hunter. His blue eyes are mesmerizing under the bright lights. "Tell us about your headband."

"It was inspired by the key lime cupcake," I say. "The volume of the bow on the hat was inspired by the frosting on the cupcakes, and I used different textured fabrics to enhance its femininity."

Hunter nods. "Good choices. I appreciate that you took inspiration from the cupcakes rather than just replicating them. Nicely done."

I let out a sigh of relief as the judges move on to Nina's barrette, which Missy calls "unique" and then Tom's heavily beaded hooded scarf, which Jasmine rules "overdone." The last designer is Curt, who was in the bottom of the pack with Tom and Luke in the zoo task. He used wool to make a cap, which looks a little plain to me.

When everyone has presented their designs, the judges leave to deliberate. Tom, Luke, and Curt finish off the last of the cupcakes while the top-five group plays cards. Beth and Zoe hold up their edible creations and vamp for the cameras. I think about approaching Daphne, but she looks like she wants to be alone. Same goes for Nina.

Oh, well, I think. Waiting for judges makes me nervous, and I'd probably say something dumb. I count the ceiling tiles instead. Before I can get too far, the judges return.

OTHER CONTESTANTS' *Designs*

DEREK'S
CUPCAKE REPLICA
FASCINATOR

MINIMAL STITCHING:
FABRIC SPRAY & GLUE GUN

ELEGANT
WITH
ATTITUDE

RACHEL'S
FLORAL APPLIQUÉD
FASCINATOR

CUPCAKE INSPIRED:
HAND-SEWN FLOWERS WITH
PEARL CENTERS

DETAILED & PRECISE

"Okay everyone, you know the drill from the last challenge," Hunter says. "Let me start by saying we were very impressed with some of your pieces."

"And much less impressed with others," Jasmine says, pointedly looking at Beth and Zoe.

"Derek," says Missy, "your design was amazing. Shane and Sam, we continue to be wowed by your creative flare. Rachel, the flowers on your design were detailed and precise. Jillian, while we differed on where your design could be worn—"

"And by whom," Jasmine mumbles.

"We were all in agreement on the skill level," Missy finishes. "You are the top five and safe for this round. Congratulations! For the next task, you'll not only have extra work time, but you'll also have the opportunity to choose a new challenge if you don't like the one you're assigned."

Sam and Shane fist bump again, but this time they bring Derek, Rachel, and Jillian into the fold.

"Unfortunately, that brings us to the bottom five," Missy says. "Two of you will have to leave us today. Daphne, while we adored your belt, the task was to make a headpiece. So, unfortunately, you are in the bottom five. And, Luke, we're afraid the cupcakes served as inspiration for your stomach rather than your design. You're also in the bottom five."

Luke smiles sheepishly and licks his lips.

"Tom," says Hunter, "we liked your idea of the hooded cloak, but the beading was way over the top."

"Which brings us to Beth and Zoe," Jasmine says. "I'm not sure what you were thinking, but it's clear you didn't take this seriously. You are both in the bottom five for this task."

I let out a sigh of relief. I wish my design was top-five worthy, but at least I'm safe for another challenge.

"I could stretch this out, but I don't think it's much of a mystery," says Hunter, looking at the bottom five. "Smashing cupcakes on material is neither avant-garde nor abstract. It's lazy. Beth, Zoe, you're both dismissed."

The girls actually giggle, which annoys me. *Why go through all the trouble of getting here if you don't care about the competition?* I wonder. Before they walk off, they blow kisses to the camera. I guess that explains it. They're just there for the cameras.

Everyone heads to the elevators, looking relieved to have survived another challenge. I'm relieved too, but I'm also a little disappointed. Being a stuck in the middle isn't good enough. I want to crack the top five.

At the elevator, Hunter taps me on the shoulder. "Chloe?"

"Yes?" I say, surprised.

"You're almost there," Hunter tells me. "Push a little harder and I think next time around a top-five spot will be yours." Before I can reply, he walks away, offering no more advice for what it is that will move me to the next level.

The next morning, I beg my mom to let me explore the city on my own. After making me promise to text her every thirty minutes, she finally gives in. Thank goodness! I need to think, but I also have a mission — I want to find Liesel McKay's store. As a previous winner *Design Diva*, I have a feeling her store will be beyond impressive. And since I met her in person back in California, thanks to her son, Jake, I feel like it's my duty to swing by. I take out the business card Jake handed me at the Santa Cruz art fair and notice the necklace he gave me is also in my purse. I put it around my neck. Maybe that's the problem — I was missing my good luck charm.

It looks like the subway will be fastest, but it's an unfamiliar maze, so I decide to walk the forty blocks to Liesel's store. That's a rookie mistake, because by the time I get there my legs are aching. After texting my mom to let her know I'm alive, I flip through the racks. There are handbags, scarves, and wraps, all adorned with Liesel's signature jewelry pieces.

If I had to choose a favorite *Design Diva* success, it would definitely be Liesel. Not only was she consistently in the top five during her season, but when the show ended, her designs became so popular and well-known that she was able to branch out and create a line of jewelry and accessories.

I keep flipping through the racks, passing over the same pieces again and again. Just then a voice says, "Find anything inspiring?" and I look up into the green eyes of Jake McKay.

"Just poking around," I say, trying to ignore the butterflies in my stomach. If I'm being honest, I was hoping I'd run into him here.

Jake takes his backpack off his shoulder and sets it on the floor. "How's the competition going?"

"It's going," I say. We're not allowed to reveal the outcomes of any of the challenges. All the contestants had to sign a confidentiality agreement when we got to New York.

"That great, huh?" Jake says.

I shrug. I'm not even allowed to tell him if I'm still in the competition or not.

"Oh, you probably can't tell me anything, can you?" Jake says. "I remember that from when my mom was on the show."

"I'm sworn to secrecy," I tell him. "Sorry, it's a little frustrating. I can't talk about anything."

Jake looks at me and snaps his fingers. "You need a change of scenery, some inspiration. Want to go for a walk?"

Suddenly legs don't ache as much as before. "Sounds good," I say. "Let me just text my mom. It's been a full eight minutes since I last checked in." I roll my eyes.

Jake laughs. "My mom was the exact same way when I first visited her in New York. It gets better."

"Visited?" I'm confused. "I thought you lived here."

"I do now," Jake replies. "But my parents are divorced, and when it first happened, I stayed with my dad so I could finish school there. My mom moved here." He swings his backpack over his shoulder, and we walk in the direction of my hotel. "Now that I go to school here, it's my mom's turn to have me all to herself."

We walk quietly for a few minutes because I'm not sure how to segue from divorce to competition strategies. Finally, Jake breaks the silence. "Smile! You're in New York! You should be excited!"

I laugh. "I am excited. It's just a little overwhelming at times." I hesitate for a second. "Can I ask you something?"

"Ask away," Jake replies.

"What was the hardest thing for your mom?" I ask. "During *Design Diva*, I mean."

Jake thinks for a minute and then says, "Probably the challenges. Some of them were pretty out there." He laughs. "For one, she had to make a collar that was inspired by Chicago's deep-dish pizza."

"I remember that episode!" I laugh. "Someone used real sauce, right?"

"Yup. Jasmine was less than thrilled," Jake says.

"The problem with crazy challenges," I begin, trying to be careful what I say, "is that it's impossible to connect to them. Like how does pizza scream fashion?"

"Well, assuming you're still in the competition," Jake says, raising an eyebrow, "think about the last round of auditions. The rodeo-inspired clothing. You had a lot of passion when you described those designs."

I throw my hands up. "Yes, because I cared about those things. How am I supposed to be passionate about peng—" I stop and clamp my hand over my mouth.

Jake grins. "Whatever task they ask you to do, you have to find a way to be passionate about it. Think of something about yourself you can bring to the challenge."

"That's easy for you to say," I mutter.

Jake looks surprised. "It sounds like you're already giving up," he says.

I stop walking. Jake's right. I do sound like I'm giving up. But I'm not. I don't think I am, anyway.

"Look," says Jake, "I'm not saying it's not hard. My mom had a really tough time with the pizza task. She was in the bottom five. But the next challenge she came back stronger than ever. You have to make that connection."

"You're right," I say quietly. My phone buzzes, and I groan. Mom, of course. "I'd better get back. My mom is freaking out." I text her that I'm on my way back to the hotel.

When I look back up from my phone, Jake is holding two mustard-covered soft pretzels. He hands me one, and I take a big bite. Yum! "Thanks for listening," I say.

"Anytime," Jake says. "You can do this — assuming you're still in the competition, that is."

I smile. "And if not, then the next time around, right?"

Jake suddenly pulls out his phone and snaps a quick picture of me. "What's your cell?"

I rattle off my number, and Jake sends me the photo. I laugh when I see the mustard on my lip. "Are you planning to sell this to the tabloids when I'm famous?" I ask.

Jake pretends to look shocked. "How did you know?"

My phone buzzes again. This time it's Hunter, telling us to meet in front of the Toys "R" Us in Times Square in one hour for our next challenge.

I sigh. Back to reality. "I have to go," I say. "Tell your mom I said hi."

"Sure thing," Jake says. "I'll text you."

"Only words of wisdom, please," I say.

"Here are the first ones," says Jake. He types something into his phone, and a moment later mine buzzes. I look down to read his text — "Make a connection."

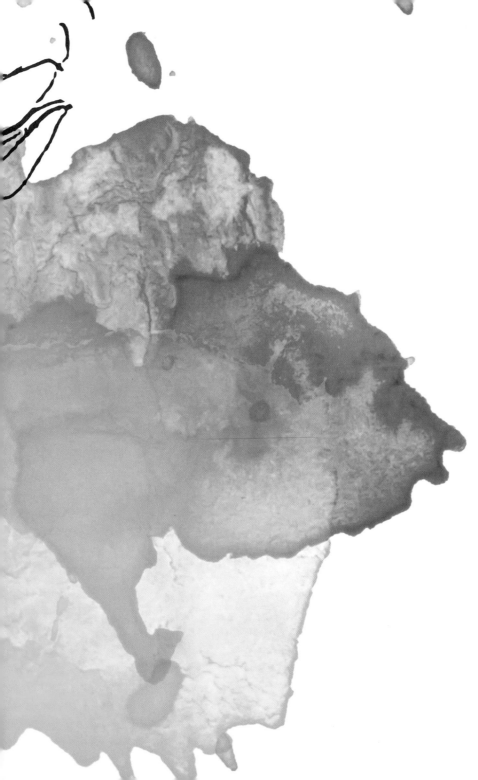

7

Times Square is like its own little world. Crowds of people swarm the blue road, which is blocked off from traffic. I push my way through and head over to Toys "R" Us, where the judges, camera crews, and some of the other designers are already waiting.

"Welcome," Jasmine says when we've all gathered around. "I have some good news for you today. Starting with this challenge, you will have access to sewing machines."

That is good news. Maybe access to a sewing machine will be what makes the difference for me in this challenge.

Jasmine looks at her watch. "It's almost one o'clock. You'll have an hour and a half to explore Toys "R" Us before you start designing."

"Needless to say," says Missy, "your next challenge will be derived from what you see. The store speakers will announce when it's time to regroup for the challenge instructions."

With that, Hunter opens the doors, and all the designers run into the store. It's enormous — at least three levels high. I follow the sound of roaring, and in minutes, I'm standing in front of a massive dinosaur replica straight out of *Jurassic Park*. It stalks and roars amid a backdrop of mountains and forest, striking fear in passing children. I take a picture with my cell, and move on to a Lego exhibit, almost bumping into the Incredible Hulk. He's bigger than as I am and made entirely of Legos. I snap another photo. He's so detailed — I can't forget those little touches in my designs too.

Candy Land is my next stop. There are giant candy canes and sugarplums just like in the board game and bin after bin of candy. While I'm debating what color jellybeans to buy, my eyes wander to the center of the store. As soon as I see the massive Ferris wheel, I know where I'll be spending the rest of my time.

The Ferris wheel sits smack in the middle of the store. The line to get on is long, but I snag a spot. I need to experience this ride. Every car on the wheel is unique. There's one that looks like a taxi, another built to resemble a school bus, and some that have movie characters. No two are alike. When it's my turn, I choose the one with Mr. Potato Head. It sails into the air, and I can see all the parts of the store. I snap more photos and think about the Ferris wheel that's erected at the fair back home every summer. It's one of my favorite times of year.

By the time the Ferris wheel touches back down, I'm inspired. I sit in a corner, flip through my photos, and jot down ideas in my sketchpad. When I hear the announcement for the designers to return to the front of the store, I'm calm. Whatever spin the judges put on this, I'm ready.

I look down at the text from Jake again. Connection made.

* * *

"I'll keep it short and sweet since I'm sure you're all eager to get started," Hunter says. "The theme of this challenge is 'The World Is a Toy Store.' Interpret that however you want, but be sure to use one or more store sections as a starting point." He takes out a box with slips of paper inside. "The item you will have to design is on these slips of paper. Take one, but don't open it."

We each take a paper. "Derek, Sam, Shane, Jillian, and Rachel — you were all in the top five last week, so you may open your papers first," Hunter continues. "As part of your prize, you have the opportunity to switch garments. But keep in mind that there is no guarantee you'll like the alternative better. So how about it? Does anyone want to switch?"

Four contestants shake their head no. Only Derek raises his hand. "I'd like to switch," he says. "With Chloe."

Me?! I think frantically. *But he doesn't even know what I have! How is he so sure it's better?* But there's nothing I can do. I frown and hand over my paper.

"You will have three hours to complete this task," Hunter says. "Last week's top-five designers will get a thirty-minute head start to choose fabrics and start designing. When they're done, the rest of you may start. The clock starts now."

The top five immediately start sketching. I look down at my new slip of paper and try to get back in my happy zone. No matter what it says, I can do it. There's no wall separating us from the top five today, and I watch them sort through the materials. When I see something with potential, I make a mental note to remember where it is. Finally, just as Derek sits down at a sewing machine, Hunter calls, "And go!" to the remaining six designers.

We race over to the sewing machines. I place my sketchpad and phone beside me before opening the slip of paper. SKIRT. That's perfect! The Ferris wheel reminded me so much of the fair back home, and with Candy Land added in, I have the perfect inspiration for my skirt — cotton candy!

Even though the top five got to choose fabrics first, the shelves are still fully stocked. I spot a bolt of tulle in a pastel pink. That's perfect for my cotton-candy skirt. I'll need a lot of yardage to create the volume I'm looking for, so I grab the entire bolt, plus a pink knit for the lining. Then I grab some three-inch-wide elastic. I'll use that to create a cinched waistband to contrast the volume of the skirt. Finally, I grab some sparkly stones and gems to add some embellishments to the skirt and tie in the whimsy of the toy-store theme.

TOYS "R" US
FINAL
Sketch

BLACK RIBBING

WHITE KNIT TOP

BIG
Pink tulle
"Cotton Candy"
skirt

Hand beaded

Whimsical Feel to Design

FERRIS WHEEL!!

It's time to get to work on the tulle. I measure and cut eight knee-length pieces of tulle so my skirt will have plenty of volume — that's key for my cotton-candy inspiration. Then I cut the pink knit lining so that it's the same length as the tulle and as wide as the hips on my dress form plus about ten inches.

Keeping an eye on the time, I get to work on the hem of my skirt. I sew the short sides of each tulle layer together using a French seam to keep the edges looking nice. Then I do the same with the lining.

An hour down, two to go. Around me, sewing machines are whirring. I'm almost at that point, but I want to get it just right. I could make a no-sew tulle skirt, but I want to take advantage of the machines. A hack job isn't going to cut it.

Next I match up the seams and top edges so I can baste the layers of tulle together. It's a painstaking process, since it's hard to see each individual layer of tulle when they're all on top of each other, but it's important to get it right.

Be patient, I remind myself. *Take your time.*

Once all the tulle is basted into one piece, I pleat and pin the top edge so it's the same width as the lining. I alternate sides so the pleats are even. Then I match up the top edges of the tulle and lining and baste the two together to hold them in place temporarily.

I quickly measure the waist of my mannequin at the narrowest part and cut a piece of elastic to fit. My skirt is meant to be high-waisted, so I want a snug fit. Putting the two cut ends together, I race over to a sewing machine and stitch them together to create an unbroken circle of elastic.

Time to put the two pieces together. I grab my skirt and some pins and mark half-, quarter-, and eighth-inch measurements around the top of the skirt and the elastic, then pin the waistband to the fabric at the marks. Finally it's time to sew. I hold the elastic and tulle together and put the pieces through the machine. They go in easily, which is such a relief from the painstaking stitching I had to do on the previous tasks. In minutes, the fabric is sewed, and I examine the neat threading. I'll never take a sewing machine for granted again!

"Forty-five minutes!" Jasmine calls.

Crunch time. I grab the gems I selected and start attaching them to the tulle. I sew them on, being careful not to rip or tear the fragile material. I place a greater concentration of gems and studs at the top of the skirt, near the waistband, and gradually lessen the embellishments as I move down the skirt, creating a cascading effect.

With fifteen minutes left, I slip the finished skirt over the top of the dress form and step back. It looks exactly as I imagined. The fullness of the skirt reminds me of the soft cotton candy I buy every year at the fair back home, and the added gemstones cascading down from the cinched waistband give it a fun, whimsical feel.

For the first time since I arrived in New York, I feel confident. This is my winning piece.

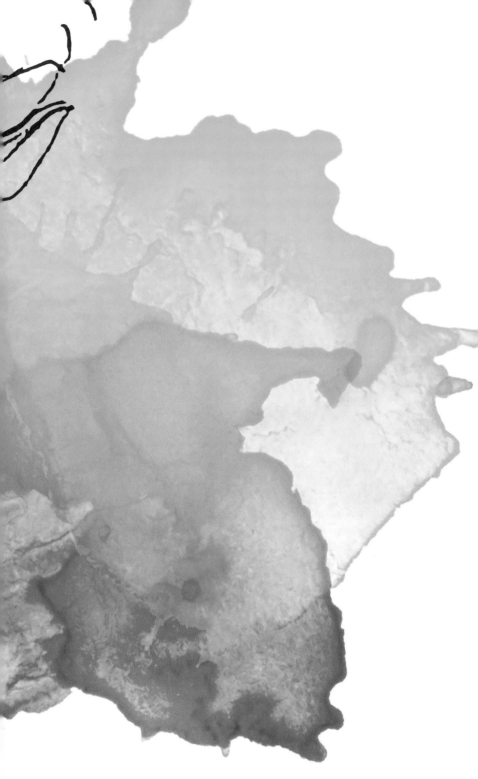

8

Jasmine moves from one design to the next, looking them up and down silently. She pauses at each one, jots something down on a piece of paper, and keeps going. Missy and Hunter follow her, taking their own notes. When they reach the end of the line, they look up — their signal to let us know they're ready.

"Let's start with the end of the line for a change," says Jasmine, moving to stand in front of Derek.

I haven't had a chance to peek at his design, but I've been dying to know what it was.

"You switched assignments with Chloe. How do you feel about your decision?" asks Jasmine.

"Great," Derek says. "I just wasn't in a skirt mood today. Chloe's assignment was a blouse, and I was up for the challenge. I was inspired by the *Jurassic Park* section of the store and found this army green rayon with a subtle camouflage print that represented that. The sheer, delicate fabric provides a good contrast to the pattern, and I added faux leather detailing on the shoulders to amp that up. The texture of the leather material reminds me of the giant dinosaur replica."

Jasmine feels the fabric and nods. "This is beautifully made. The material drapes so well, and I love the contrast between the sheer airy fabric and the faux leather."

Derek tips an imaginary hat in thanks, and the judges love it. I'm sure they'd be happy to stand and talk to him all day, but they move on. Tom is next, standing in front of his denim design. "My garment was a jacket, which I chose to make out of denim," he explains. "It's my nod to the Super Mario Brothers."

Jasmine studies the jacket. "The stitching is a bit obvious and I don't love with the oversized buttons, but it's fine."

Nina is next, and she's bouncing in anticipation. "I used the Ferris wheel for inspiration," she says as soon as the judges pause in front of her.

I fight the urge to roll my eyes. Great minds think alike, I guess. I just hope she doesn't have the same explanation as I do. Especially since we're from the same hometown.

"My garment was a skirt," Nina continues.

DEREK'S
TOYS "R" US
Design

LEATHER
APPLIQUÉ
SHOULDERS

CAMO PRINT

INVERTED
CENTER PLEAT

Army Green Rayon Fabric

Oh, come on! I think. *We both have skirts and chose the Ferris wheel as inspiration?* I crane my neck to see her design and breathe a sigh of relief. At least there are no similarities between our designs. Nina created a floor-length, A-line skirt in black with a red heart pattern along the hem. It reminds me of construction paper hearts from grade school. It looks so forced. Usually, her designs are more chic.

"And how did the Ferris wheel play into this?" Missy asks her.

Nina blushes. "I had my first kiss on the Ferris wheel, and I wanted people to think of love and romance when they looked at this skirt."

What? I think. *That is so not Nina — and so not true!* Nina is terrified of Ferris wheels. I know for a fact that she's never even been on one. She's been terrified of heights ever since we were kids. I narrow my eyes, and she smirks. Anything to win, huh? I think back to Nina elbowing me during the last challenge. That seems much less of an accident now.

"Awww!" Missy exclaims. "That's so sweet!" I have to fight the urge to gag.

Once the judges have gotten their dose of Nina's artificial sweetness, they move over to the two sets of twins. All four designers are sitting beside each other and whispering.

"Girls," Hunter says, frowning, "it's completely possible that you both got dresses but—"

Jillian's face reddens as she interrupts Hunter. "We did both get dresses! I swear!"

"Fine, I'm willing to give you the benefit of the doubt on that," Hunter says. "But I find it incredibly hard to believe that you each independently chose to make dresses with drawstring belts."

Rachel turns red. "We're twins. We have a sixth sense."

Jillian seems to sense things aren't going well. "We, um, also both chose Candy Land as our inspiration," she mumbles. "But it was total coincidence."

Luke laughs, but is quickly silenced by Jasmine's killer stare. "This twinsy cuteness may have been fine if these designs were spectacular," she says. "Unfortunately, the pink beading and sequins look like a birthday cake exploded."

The girls' lips quiver at Jasmine's harsh words, and Jillian wipes at her eyes with the back of her hand. It's clear the sisters thought their designs were stellar.

Jasmine moves over to Sam and Shane, her lip curled in a sneer. I imagine the producers using a close-up shot of that angry face for promos. "Do you and your brother have a sixth sense as well?" she asks sarcastically.

Shane looks shaken. "Sometimes, but not today," he says. He presents a pair of red corduroy pants. I'm not usually a huge fan of corduroy, but I have to admit the bold red fabric he chose makes them look cool and modern.

"I was inspired by the superhero section," Shane explains. "Superheroes are clearly special, but they try to blend in among us. When I was designing, I thought about how I've been working to blend in here and tried to combine the elements of my home state of Texas with the originality of New York style."

Hunter, Missy, and Jasmine look at the pants from all sides. Finally Missy breaks the silence. "You didn't just try," she says, beaming, "you succeeded!"

Shane lets out a sigh, clearly relieved. Sam, on the other hand, is visibly sweating as he presents his vest. "I used the *Toy Story* section for inspiration since I love working with denim," he says nervously. "I added leather fringe to the hem to give it a cowboy feel but kept the top simple and clean."

Even Jasmine seems to have pity for him. "Thank you, Sam. You can relax." She waves to one of the producers, who brings over a cup of water.

By the time the judges get to me, I just want to be done. It's been a long day. Hunter speaks first. "Chloe, I'm impressed. This skirt is not something I would have expected from you. The color and design both seem like a big departure from your usual style."

"They are," I agree. "I'm usually a bit more minimalist and drawn to neutral colors. But I was inspired to try something new this challenge."

TOYS "R" US
FINAL
Design

COLOR PALETTE:
PINK, BLACK,
& WHITE

WHIMSICAL FEEL
TO DESIGN

SKIRT WITH
VOLUME & SPARKLE

Cotton-Candy-Inspired Design

Missy nods. "And you were inspired by?"

"The Ferris wheel," I say. Nina snorts, but I ignore her. "It reminded me of the fair held back home every summer. And one of my favorite things about the fair, aside from riding the Ferris wheel, is eating cotton candy, which is what inspired my skirt. I also spent some time in the store's Candy Land section, so that helped too. I was going for a whimsical feel, since that's what toy stores are really all about. I think the volume of the skirt and the scattered gems create that."

"Very impressive," Hunter says. I smile, but the judges are already moving on to Daphne.

"What happened?" asks Missy, unable to control her surprise at Daphne's misshapen blouse.

Daphne throws her hands up helplessly. "The sewing machine and I had a fight. It won." She scrunches the pretty turquoise material in her hands as she talks. It's obvious how beautiful the blouse could have been.

The judges peer closely at the stitching. I'm sure there are good things about the shirt, but it looks so wrinkled and frayed, it's practically impossible to tell. There's nothing Daphne can do at this point, and she hangs her head as the judges walk away to decide our fashion fate once again.

The judges are gone longer than usual this time. I'm not sure if that's good or bad. Either they're having a hard time deciding between all the good designs, or they think everything was so bad it's impossible for them to choose. Finally, after almost an hour of deliberating, they reappear.

"Thank you for waiting," Jasmine says. "After much discussion, we have reached our decision. We thought having access to sewing machines this week would make things easier for you, but it seems we were wrong. Many of you struggled with this challenge. That's why this week we'll only have a top two, rather than a top five."

"Now on to the good news," Missy says, seeming eager to get things back on a more positive note. "Derek, it was a risky move to switch garments with Chloe, but it paid off. You're one of our top two designers this week."

Hunter steps forward. "It paid off for more than just you," he says. "We have a new addition joining the top of the pack today. Chloe, you stepped outside your comfort zone and took this challenge to heart with your cotton-candy skirt. Well done. You're the other designer in the top two."

I can hardly believe it. I finally did it! "Thank you," I say. I want to scream and cheer and hug everyone around me, but we're not done. I have to be content with an excited grin.

"Of course with a top we must also have a bottom," says Hunter. "Luke, while we admire the ambition you showed in trying something different, the short time frame doesn't leave time for any type of tie-dye. Your design clearly wasn't very thought-out. Therefore, you're in the bottom five."

Luke's face falls as he drops a handful of soggy paper towels onto the floor. I can't fault the judges for their critique — dye is still dripping off Luke's top.

"Joining him today is Daphne," Jasmine says. "I can certainly picture what the blouse could have been. The color was gorgeous, and I would have liked to have seen the finished product. Unfortunately, the sewing machine was your downfall today."

Daphne looks like she's trying not to cry as Jasmine turns to Rachel and Jillian. "Girls, not only were your designs almost identical — which is a clear violation — they also looked lazy. It was clear you didn't give much, if any, thought to their execution. You're also in the bottom five."

"And rounding out our bottom five is Nina," Missy says. "We know you tried to show romance with your skirt, but I'm afraid the hearts along the hem came across as amateur. They didn't match the feel of the rest of the skirt and took away from the garment's sophistication."

I see Nina clench her fists. Clearly she thought her story about her Ferris wheel first kiss would be enough to win over the judges.

"There's no need to draw this out," Hunter says. "Nina, Daphne, and Luke, you're safe today. Rachel and Jillian, it's clear you broke the rules by making identical designs. You will be leaving us today."

As Jillian and Rachel sniffle and start to say their goodbyes, Derek leans over and smiles at me. "Welcome to the top," he whispers. I can hardly believe it. My design has finally broken away from the middle of the pack.

Looks like Jake's advice paid off big time — making a connection was enough to propel me to the top.

"To your first big win," says Mom, raising her glass toward me as we celebrate over dinner that night.

"Why thank you," I say, clinking glasses.

Mom smiles. "Glad you're in a better mood," she says."Just remember, there are still several challenges left. I'm not saying you won't always be in the top, but it's possible. And I don't want one bad day making you doubt yourself, okay?"

"Okay," I say. "I'll do my best. Now can we focus on the happy part of this conversation?"

"Absolutely!" Mom says with a smile.

But just then my phone buzzes. I look at the screen and see it's a text from Hunter. "You have to be kidding me!" I exclaim. "We already had a challenge today."

"Maybe he's congratulating everyone for making it this far," Mom suggests.

I roll my eyes. "Doubtful." I open my phone and read his message. "'Congratulations to all who've made it this far!'"

"See!" Mom says. "What did I tell you?"

"Don't say 'I told you so' yet," I warn. "There's more."

I scroll down to read the rest of Hunter's text. "'The competition is getting fierce, and our next task is right around the corner. Literally. Meet us at ACE Hardware at eight p.m. sharp for the next challenge.'"

* * *

When I get to the hardware store around the corner from our hotel, something is different. It takes me a minute to realize what it is. Then it hits me: Unlike before the previous challenges, no one looks happy to be here. Except for the judges maybe.

"I know none of you anticipated this next challenge so soon, but we like to keep you on your toes," Missy says. "After all, spontaneity is part of the fashion world."

"And ratings," someone mumbles.

Hunter grins. "Ratings are important for the show, but they also help you. In two challenges, we'll be down to the final five. In the next stages of the competition, having the opportunity to show your designs will be that much more important. The more the audience hears about and sees your designs, the better for you. Trust me."

The skin on my arms tingles. I think back to the *Design Diva* competitions Alex and I have watched. In past seasons, the final five had their designs displayed in Macy's and Saks store windows. One season, a challenge prize was a spread in Vogue. I would freak out if I won something half that good.

"For today," says Missy, "all that matters is this elimination task. You will be divided into three teams. Two contestants from the losing team will be let go. This challenge will require you to think outside the box since you'll be using some unique materials — either duct tape or newspaper. You can use other supplies from around the store as well, but one of those materials must make up the majority of your garment."

Around me, I hear the other designers grumbling. I don't blame them. I've seen some creative prom dresses made out of duct tape, but I certainly never expected to be making a real garment out of the material. Let alone old newspaper.

"To keep things fair, your teams will be chosen randomly," Hunter says, passing around a basket full of folded slips of paper. "Everyone have a number? Good. All the ones stand by Jasmine. Twos, by Missy. Threes, to my right."

All the designers shuffle to our designated places. My stomach drops as my group comes together: me, Nina, and Daphne. I'm not happy about it, but Nina and I have faked nice before. And if it means winning a challenge, I can do anything.

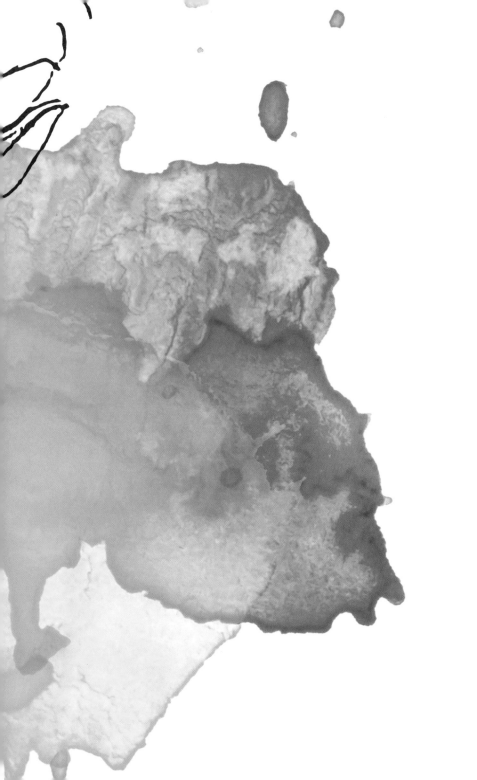

10

"You will have one hour to plan your design and gather materials and two hours to make it," says Hunter. "You must decide as a group how you want to split up the duties. If it's best for each group member to work on his or her strength, that's fine. If you'd rather all work together, that's fine too. No aisle is off limits. You may begin."

Nina, Daphne, and I stare at each other for a moment. It's clear no one is quite sure where to begin. Then Daphne takes out her notebook and pencil. "Okay, let's get started. We need to figure out whether we're using tape or newspaper and figure out a design."

"I vote for newspaper," I say. "It'll be easier to work with than duct tape. We could do a cool structured dress. Maybe with a pencil skirt or peplum or something. Or we could crinkle the paper to add volume and texture."

"I think we should add some color to it," Nina says. "Otherwise it's going to be too boring."

"We don't have time," I remind her. "Even if we could find the supplies to dye it, there's no time to let it dry. We'd be stuck with soaking wet newspaper. Remember what happened to Luke last challenge?"

Nina looks irritated, but Daphne nods in agreement. "Good point," she says. "Let's just focus on making something really structural and detailed. I think that's a better use of our time."

"I disagree," Nina says.

"Well, this isn't the Nina group," Daphne replies.

Nina stares coldly at her. I've seen that look before, when one of her followers back home dared to disagree with her. The difference now is that Daphne doesn't back down. *Maybe she's someone to be reckoned with after all*, I think.

* * *

After twenty minutes, we've managed to come up with a design — a structured, strapless dress with a pencil skirt and flared peplum. We split up to grab our materials — a huge stack of newspaper, some Velcro, white thread, straight pins, and several pencils, rulers, and pairs of scissors.

I grab three full-size sheets of newspaper and stack them together evenly so all the edges are lined up. Starting at one side, I start to make pleats for the peplum, which will give our dress some visual interest and structural detailing. I use one of the rulers to measure and fold one side of the paper half an inch, then crease it to make sure it's crisp. Still moving from the same side, I make a one-inch fold, measuring carefully to make sure the pleats are straight. The bottom half of the dress depends on the structural details, so they have to be precise.

Flipping the sheets of newspaper over, I fold the paper up to meet the edge of my original half-inch crease. Then I flip the newspapers over again, create another one-inch fold, and crease it firmly. In order to make the pleats, I have to create another smaller, half-inch crease, which I fold up to meet the edge of the first half-inch fold.

When I'm done, I glance down — one pleat done, about a million to go. Luckily, Daphne and Nina are already both hard at work pleating their own stacks of newspapers too. We need them for the peplum plus the waistband and back of the pencil skirt, so it's all hands on deck to get this skirt done in time.

Once we have four sheets of pleats finished, it's time to start sewing. I measure to the center of two of the pleated pieces and draw a line in pencil to mark the spot. While I'm

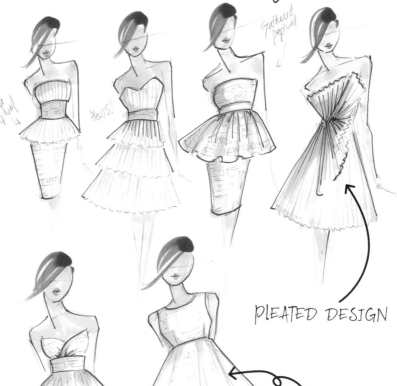

Newspaper Dress Design!!!!

Gathered peplum!

PLEATED DESIGN

FLARE SKIRT
DRESS DESIGN

TEAMWORK:
GROUP PROJECT WITH
NINA & DAPHNE

HARDWARE STORE
DEVELOPMENT
Sketches

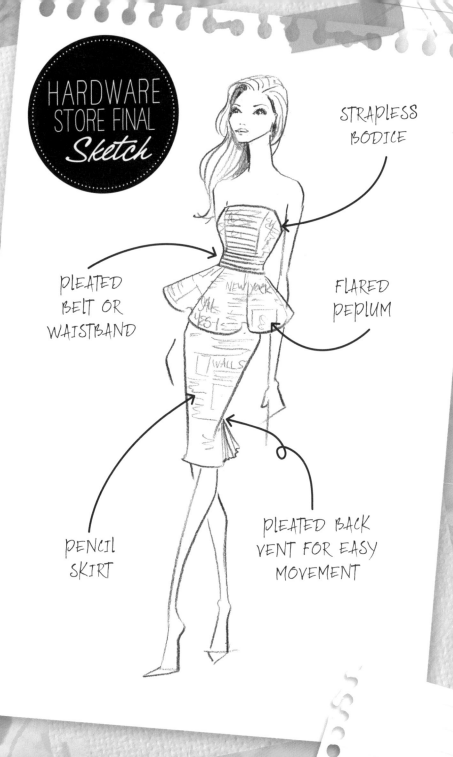

doing that, Nina measures the other two pieces and makes a mark about an inch and a half above the center point.

"We should baste them together first," Daphne says. "Or use a long stitch and a low thread tension. That way we can take the stiches out without ruining the paper if we need to."

"Good point," Nina agrees. "I don't want to have to redo all those pleats. And more importantly, we don't have time."

It's hard to believe Nina is being so agreeable. I glance at the other teams, and they seem to be working well together too. *Maybe we should have had partner tasks from the beginning*, I think. Not only are we getting way more done, but I'm much less anxious knowing we're doing this as a team — at least now that I see how well we're working.

Daphne moves to the sewing machine and Nina and I exchange a nervous look. I can tell we're both remembering her battle with the sewing machine last challenge. Daphne must sense our fear, because she glances back at us. "Don't worry, I learned my lesson last time," she says. "I've got this."

Sure enough, Daphne sews straight across the pencil lines, keeping the pleats folded as she moves the paper through the machine. Soon all four pieces have their pleats secured in place. Next Daphne grabs one of the pieces with the off-center stitching and lines up the seam with one of the center-stitched pieces, letting them overlap about half an inch. She sews the two pieces together where they overlap, then does the same thing with the other two mismatched pieces. Finally, she sews the pieces together so we have a long strip of pleated paper.

Nina grabs a length of rope to use as a belt as we move over to our dress form to fit the newspaper bodice and peplum skirt. Daphne and I wrap the pleated paper around the dress form, making sure the center stitching hits at the natural waist. Then Nina belts it to hold it in place. The three of us exchange excited grins. It's really coming together.

I grab some pins to start fitting the bodice, pressing the pleats down across the chest so they lie flat. I pin the pleats in place in front and back, and Daphne grabs a pencil to trace the neckline and a deeper, low-cut back. When we have the neckline set, we bring the bodice back over to the sewing machine and sew just below the traced line, pulling the pins out as we go. Once we're finished stitching, we cut along the traced line.

We add the Velcro closure to the back of the bodice and sew a second waist seam to help smooth the pleats. Having two seams will make the midsection lie flat and look more flattering. We put the bodice on our dress form for safekeeping. Now it's time to add the pencil skirt.

I grab three sheets of newspaper, just like I did with the pleated peplum portion of the dress, and stack them on top of each other. I baste them together quickly, then use an iron to smooth out any wrinkles. It's important for our pencil skirt to be sleek and straight in order to contrast with the flared peplum.

I sew as fast as I can, making sure to add a pleated center back vent to the bottom of the pencil skirt so the wearer can walk easily without tearing the dress. While I'm doing that, Nina and Daphne each make their own panels. Finally we connect all the bottom layers, sew them together near the top seams, and attach another piece of Velcro at the back.

"Thirty minutes!" Jasmine calls out.

Daphne, Nina, and I put the pencil skirt on the dress form and attach the pleated bodice and peplum over the top. Then we stand back to admire our work. The flared peplum stands out perfectly against the straight pencil skirt, and the neckline is perfectly fitted. But still . . .

"It needs something," Nina says. "It's too plain."

I study the dress too. I hate to admit it, but I think Nina might be right. It does need something else to take it from good to great.

Nina thinks for a minute, then snaps her fingers. "I've got it! A belt! I can make a thick one out of the pleated newspaper we have left to help define the waist."

I hear the gloating in Nina's voice. I know it's petty, but I hate that she's the one to come up with the idea. And I know she'll make sure everyone knows it.

Nina races away to grab more newspaper. I see her flipping through sheets of pleated paper until she finds what she's looking for — a section that's darker than all the rest.

"Fifteen minutes!" the judges announce.

Nina runs the belt through the machine and attaches a piece of Velcro at the back. "Done!" she hollers. She hurries back to the mannequin and adds the belt to our design.

I have to admit, it's perfect. The dark newspaper looks like a wide black belt cinching in the waist of the dress. There's no way one person could have gotten this much done in the time limit. This dress was truly a team effort. I can only hope it was a winning effort as well.

As the three teams assemble in front of the judges, I see
that it's not just our group that's huddled together. Everyone
seems to have bonded over this team task.

"First of all, let me begin by saying how impressed we
are with the creativity of all the designs," says Hunter. "No
one just slapped something together and called it art. You
all made something unique and wearable out of unusual
materials."

"I think I'd wear all three of these designs," Missy adds
cheerfully.

"I don't know if I'd go *quite* that far," Jasmine says with
a little laugh.

"Let's start with group one," says Hunter, walking
over to Derek, Luke, and Sam. They've created a high-

low skirt with a chevron pattern entirely out of duct tape. "Great work, guys. I love the striking contrast between the black and white, and the chevron pattern you chose is very modern."

Jasmine moves around the dress form, examining the skirt from all angles. "It looks like you had a little bit of trouble in the back here. The lines don't seem to be as straight as they do in the front of the skirt. And they're a bit uneven."

"We had some difficulty getting the different sections measured precisely to line up our pattern," Derek admits quietly.

"That was was my fault," says Sam, looking down at his feet. "I misjudged the pattern in the back, and it threw things off a bit."

"But we all came together in the end to make it work and created a wearable skirt," Luke says, clearly trying to end on a positive note.

"Thank you," says Hunter. "Missy, do you want to discuss group two's design?"

"Love to!" Missy says, walking over to Shane, Curt, and Tom. They've created a dress with a full skirt made out of garbage bags and a strapless top out of black duct tape. Even from here, I can tell that it's not as sophisticated as group one's skirt.

We're the only group that went with newspaper, I realize. Hopefully that risk is a good thing. Maybe it will set us apart.

Missy examines the dress. "I like the look of this dress. The full skirt is very fun, and I like the varying proportions between that and the more fitted top. I could definitely see this as a party dress."

"Can I say something about it?" Jasmine asks. She doesn't wait for a response. "I appreciate the concept, but this skirt is seriously lacking in construction. It's all taped and scrunched; no sewing involved. And the skirt is really the focal point of your garment, not the duct-tape top. That'd be fine if the challenge hadn't been to use duct tape or newspaper for the majority of the garment."

"Curt made the skirt!" Tom mutters, just loud enough for the judges to hear.

"What's your problem, dude?" says Curt, shooting his teammate an irritated look. "You're the one who wanted to make the skirt out of trash bags."

Jasmine glances over at Shane for confirmation. "Well?" she says.

"Uh, yeah," Shane says, looking uncomfortable at being put in the middle. "It was Tom's idea, but Curt did most of the skirt construction."

"And where exactly do you fit in here, Shane?" Jasmine asks him.

OTHER CONTESTANTS' *Designs*

BLACK DUCT TAPE BODICE

FULL SKIRT

TEAMWORK: DRESS BY SHANE, CURT, & TOM

Glam Hardware Store Look

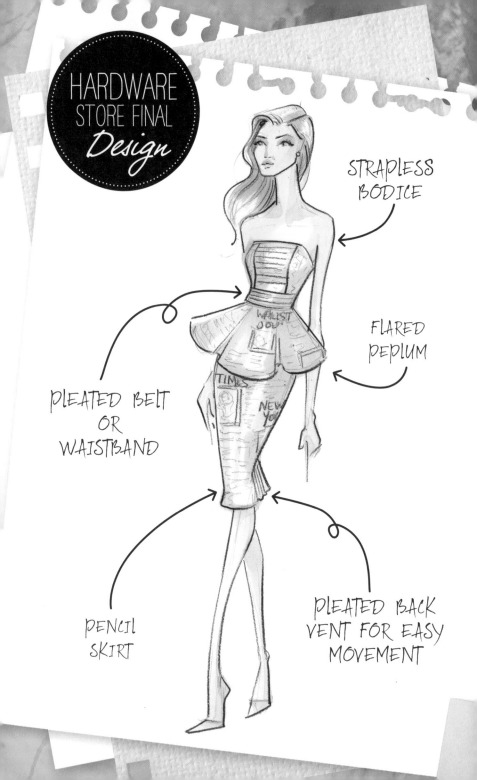

"I, um, was in charge of the top," Shane says. "I wanted to create a fitted top to contrast with the fullness of the skirt, and the black duct tape reminded me of patent leather, which is why I chose it."

Jasmine looks at him for a moment, and Shane seems to be holding his breath as he awaits her judgement. "Good choice," Jasmine finally says.

Shane lets out an audible sigh of relief as the judges move toward our group. Daphne, Nina, and I are all still holding hands. My fingers are starting to get sweaty, but I don't let go of my teammates.

"Girls, I have to say, I'm impressed," Missy says. "You're the only group that chose to use newspaper for this challenge, and it really paid off. This dress is unique and beautiful."

"I agree," Hunter adds. "I'm glad to see one of the groups chose newspaper. It works well with the detail of your design."

Even Jasmine seems to be a fan. "I like the focus you've put on the natural waist of the dress," she says, stepping forward to inspect our creation.

Nina is quick to speak up and take credit. "That was my idea," she says with a proud smile. "I thought the dress needed something to contrast the peplum and create added definition at the waist."

Knowing the cameras are on me, I have to fight the urge to roll my eyes. *Just keep smiling*, I think. *If we win, it won't matter that Nina took all the credit. At least she didn't throw you under the bus.*

"Good choice," says Jasmine.

"I'm all about doing what's best for the team," Nina says sweetly. I grit my teeth at her fake team-player attitude but don't say anything.

Jasmine walks around the dress and examines the stitching and pleating. "Very nice," she finally says. "I have to say, I was not expecting this." Her face is serious, and I can't tell what she means. From the bewildered looks on Nina's and Daphne's faces, neither can they.

Finally the judges finish examining our dress and gather to deliberate.

"I think that went well," I whisper to my teammates. "What do you guys think?"

"We'll see," says Nina.

There's a lot of nodding and head shaking as the judges discuss the three designs. I try to read their lips, but Missy sees me looking and covers her mouth with her hand. Oh, well. I was never good at lip-reading anyway.

"What do you think they're saying?" Daphne asks.

"That they're never seen anyone as talented as our group," I joke.

Nina snorts. "I wish."

I rub my eyes. Between the last challenge and this one, I'm exhausted. Today feels like it will never end. Finally, the judges seem to come to a decision.

Hunter walks over to the three groups again. "Thank you for your patience," he says. "We didn't want to make our decision in haste."

"You all did a fine job, but there was one group that exceeded our expectations," says Jasmine. "There were minor issues, but overall the design went above and beyond in terms of skill and creativity. Group three, congratulations. All three of you are safe tonight!"

Group three? That's us! Nina, Daphne, and I all squeal and hug. But we don't have much time to celebrate. There's still an elimination to go.

"This means," Jasmine continues, "groups one and two, one of you is the bottom group. Tom, Shane, Curt, unfortunately, your dress just wasn't up to par tonight. The challenge was to use duct tape or newspaper, and you instead chose to focus on trash bags. What's more, your skirt construction was lacking. Tom and Curt, I'm sorry, but you'll both be leaving us."

Tom and Curt shake hands with the judges and say their goodbyes to the other boys, who look sad to see them go. The seven of us who are still in the competition high-five happily. Nina, Daphne, and I laugh as we duck from the twins' fist bumps. When we get to the hotel, we say goodbye and head to our rooms.

I can't wait to crawl into bed. After tonight's challenge, I'll need my rest. After all, who knows what tomorrow will bring? I've managed to move from the middle to the top, but knowing this competition, staying there will be the real challenge.

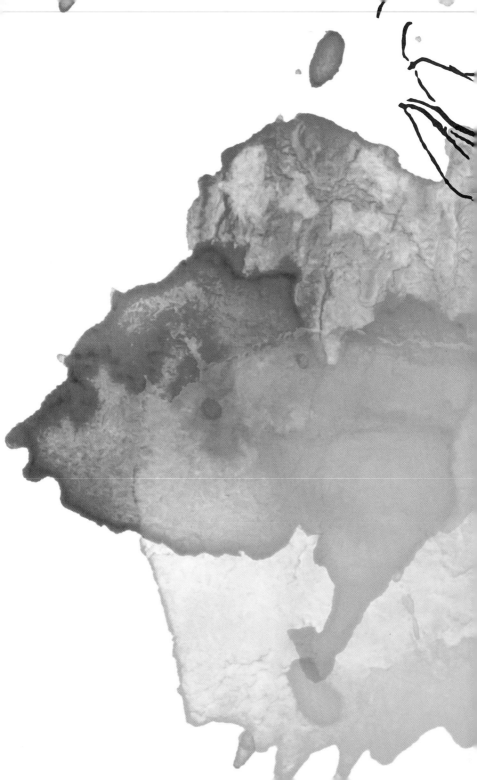

Author Bio

MARGIE

Margaret Gurevich has wanted to be a writer since second grade. She has written for many magazines and currently writes young adult and middle grade books. She loves hiking, cooking, reading, watching too much television, and spending time with her husband and son.

Illustrator Bio

BROOKE

Brooke Hagel is a fashion illustrator based in New York City. While studying fashion design at the Fashion Institute of Technology, she began her career as an intern, working in the wardrobe department of *Sex and the City*, the design studios of Cynthia Rowley, and the production offices of *Saturday Night Live*. After graduating, Brooke began designing and styling for Hearst Magazines, contributing to *Harper's Bazaar*, *House Beautiful*, *Seventeen*, and *Esquire*. Brooke is now a successful illustrator with clients including *Vogue*, *Teen Vogue*, *InStyle*, Dior, Brian Atwood, Hugo Boss, Barbie, Gap, and Neutrogena.